The Christmas Tree

JULIE SALAMON

Illustrated by Jill Weber

Random House Trade Paperbacks / New York

2002 Random House Trade Paperback Edition

Copyright © 1996 by Julie Salamon & Jill Weber
All rights reserved under International Pan-American Copyright
Conventions. Published in the United States by Random House
Trade Paperbacks, a division of Random House, Inc., New York,
and simultaneously in Canada by Random House
of Canada Limited, Toronto.

RANDOM HOUSE TRADE PAPERBACKS and colophon are trademarks
of Random House, Inc.

This work was originally published in hardcover by Random House, Inc.,
in 1996.

Salamon, Julie.
The Christmas Tree / by Julie Salamon : illustrated by Jill Weber.
p.   cm.
Summary: At Christmastime, a nun agrees to donate to
Rockefeller Center a fir tree which has been her best friend
since the time she arrived at her convent as a young orphan.

ISBN 0-375-76108-X
[1. Christmas—Fiction.   2. Trees—Fiction.   3. Orphans—Fiction.
4. Nuns—Fiction.]   I. Weber, Jill, ill.   II. title.
PZ7.S1474Ch   1996b
[Fic]--dc20   96-19052

Designed by Jill Weber

Random House website address: www.atrandom.com

Printed in the United States of America

246897531

For our children

Roxie and Eli
Salamon-Abrams
and
Remy Weber

Acknowledgments

Special thanks to Bill Clegg, who lit the spark and tended it with great care, to Elsa Burt for her enthusiasm and help, and to Ann Godoff, Kathy Robbins, Janis Donnaud, and Stacy Rockwood. This has been an affectionate collaboration, and our husbands, Bill Abrams and Frank Weber, have been a loving part of it, as have Barbara and Lew Schwartz, Arthur and Lilly Salcman, and Bud and Marge Abrams. We'd also like to thank Sister Stephen and the others at the Carmel Richmond Nursing Home in Staten Island for helping a dear friend, Bruna Alpini; Sister Sarah of the Corpus Christi Monastery in the Bronx; and David Murbach, manager of the gardens division at Rockefeller Center, who thoughtfully explained the ins-and-outs of finding the perfect Christmas tree. We love Christmas at Rockefeller Center so, though we've never met the Sisters of Christian Charity in Mendham, New Jersey, we appreciated their gift of a tree in 1995, which touched our hearts and imagination and led us to create our story and pictures.

The Christmas Tree

PROLOGUE

$\mathcal{I}$'m not a sentimental man, but when I saw her standing there, under the Christmas tree at Rockefeller Center, I started to cry.

She was not a young woman; in fact, she was fairly old. But her eyes stayed fixed on the star at the top of the tree with the curiosity and amazement of a child who has just discovered something new and wonderful. With her bright, bony face barely poking out of her black habit she looked like a little bird next to that giant tree. Only later would I understand exactly what lay behind the sparkle in her eyes, what it all meant to her.

Her name was Sister Anthony, and she was a friend of mine.

An unlikely friend, I suppose. I'm still not sure she ever knew what she did for me. But that's how it goes, I guess. You're touched by something or someone here and react to it over there and most times you don't connect one thing to the other. With Sister Anthony I knew, and I am grateful for that.

Forgive me. I'm getting ahead of myself. Let me tell you who I am and how I found myself in tears at an event that had become routine for me long ago.

I am the chief gardener at Rockefeller Center, though I think of myself as a magician of sorts. It's up to me to conjure up a Christmas tree every year—a tree so grand, so impressive—so magical—that it can stop New Yorkers in their tracks. If you've ever seen people flying around Manhattan, especially at Christmas, you can appreciate why I always get a little nervous this time of year.

It's enough to make you dread the season. We've had so many perfect trees perfection has become the norm. When you get 100 out of 100 every year you get no praise for getting 100 again, only complaints if you don't.

What is perfection?

It's hard to describe exactly what makes the perfect Christmas tree. The physical requirements are straightforward enough. The tree must stand tall and straight. Its branches must be thick and graceful, and they must point upward, giving the impression that they are reaching to the sky. They also have to be flexible, since they are tied down during the long journey to New York City.

But the trees that are finally selected need something more than height, thickness and suppleness—even more than mere beauty. And that's where I come in. I'm not an exceptional fellow in most ways, but I do have this gift. I can see if a tree has character, a spirit that outshines the ornaments and tinsel and lights—if its beauty comes from the inside and not just the outside.

I don't know how to put it any other way. I've often wished I had the same gift with people.

Walk through any park and you'll be able to find them, if you look for the right signs. In summer, the grass around their trunks will be flattened and brown because so many people have sat there. In winter, you feel warmer just looking at them; the wind seems to stop when it comes their way. They are contradictory, these trees: gigantic and sturdy, yet gentle and comforting. It has something to do with the way they hold their branches.

We've had a white spruce now and again over the years and there were a couple of Douglas firs, but that was before my time. Usually, though, we've had our best luck with Norway spruces. They're nice and green, not like the Colorado spruces, which have a blue tint. Sometimes when I'm asked why so many of the Christmas trees have been Norway spruces I'll make up a story about how they've got the right spirit because they grow so close to the North Pole. People like that.

But the real reason isn't quite so romantic. The real reason is that Norway spruces are easy to find. And they grow pretty fast, for an evergreen tree.

You wouldn't catch me planting them, though. They don't live all that long. They can start getting ragged and broken when they're as young as thirty, just when other trees are hitting their stride. Although that hasn't seemed to bother anyone else. Norway spruces were brought here by the Germanic people of Northern

Europe when they settled the Northeast, maybe for sentimental reasons. And people have been planting them ever since.

Even so, the search for the Christmas tree can take a long time. I start looking for next year's tree before this year's tree is lit. I never want to relive the year we didn't find the tree until September. That might not seem late at all, but Christmas is a very big deal at Rockefeller Center. The preparations alone are enormous. We have these super-giant ornaments that take a week *each* to install, not to mention the mountains of pinecones and bells we put up all over the place, the giant toy soldiers, the poinsettias. You can get lost in Christmas.

I have people scouting for me in all the states around New York, even as far as Canada. They call me when they think they've found the tree and after they've checked with the owners, who couldn't be more delighted to have us come and take away this giant monster growing in their backyard before it falls and breaks through their roof.

I always go to check it out, even though I know before I go this probably won't be the one. But you have to go, because the one tree you overlook is sure to be it.

No matter where I go, I'm always looking for the tree. Sometimes I take a helicopter; I can cover half a county in a day. But most often I'm in my car. As I drive along I keep one eye on the road, and one eye in the sky, hoping to see that tantalizing bit of green, that mysterious mixture of majesty and magic. Sometimes when I've been on the road too long I imagine the trees are waving to me, calling me over.

For a minute I feel exhilarated. *I've found it*, I'll think. But then I have to figure out how to reach that seductive treetop. A lot of times the tree is in some-body's backyard in a suburb filled with one-way streets. You can spend an hour circling around trying to find this beautiful thing. Then, when you get there, you discover the bottom's a mess. It's jammed up against a wall or has been ruined by trimming.

Other times, I may find the right tree—but that turns out to be only the beginning. This may sound peculiar, but sometimes the search for the Christmas tree feels a little like an old-fashioned courtship. A lot of people grow very attached to their trees. They love them. I've been amazed to discover the hold a tree can have on a person. I have learned to wait for the moment when, for one reason or another, the owners are ready to part with their trees—and that can take years.

Why am I telling you this?

Well, I've seen where the Christmas trees come from. I've seen them when they were glorious without a single ornament on them. But like most of us I've been so busy getting to where I'm going I haven't had a lot of time to think about where I've been. It only hit me, how lucky I am, that day at Rockefeller Center, when I realized I would never look at the Christmas tree—or my life, for that matter—the same way again.

Which brings me back to Sister Anthony.

Chapter One
BRUSH CREEK

 We'd flown over half of New Jersey, it felt like, and we were ready to call it a day. Not a single one of the trees I'd been told about had come even close to what we needed. I was barely paying attention by then, just enough to notice that this was one of the prettiest parts of the state. The landscape was lush and green, scarcely populated.

My head was nodding and I was just about to doze off. Then something made me sit up and look hard at the ground. For a second I couldn't tell if I was awake or asleep, I was so tired. But as my head cleared I knew I wasn't dreaming. There it was! No question about it.

This tree was a star. Everything about it said so: its rich color, the regal way it held itself—even where it stood, just apart from a whole group of evergreens, as if it was special.

"Can you go down a little?" I shouted over the noise of the chopper.

I held my breath. Usually closer inspection means disappointment. Half the branches are floppy, or the tree holds them too stiff.

Not this tree. It seemed to have that improbable combination I was looking for—the size of King Kong and the suppleness of Giselle.

My eyes wandered over the surrounding terrain, and settled on a large, elegant building.

"Do you know who owns this place?" I asked the pilot.

He glanced at a map. "That's what I thought," he said.

"What is it?" I asked, impatiently.

"Nuns own it," he said. "This is the Brush Creek convent."

"A convent?" I said. "Isn't this a little plush?"

The pilot was a New Jersey boy and knew his way around.

"This is no ordinary convent," he began.

I interrupted. "I can see that," I said.

He was nicer than I was, ignored my wise-guy rudeness.

"Brush Creek was modeled after the grand estates of Europe," he said, with the polish of a tour guide. "The man who built it wanted his children to see beauty wherever they looked and he had the means to do it. So the place has all kinds of orchards and pretty little valleys and woods. From what I've heard, sounds like he was an interesting guy—besides making everything look nice, he started experimenting with conservation long before most people knew what the word meant. They say the house has so many windows that no matter where you go in it, you feel the pull of nature. He named it Brush Creek after the little stream that runs through the middle."

He studied the map more closely, then pointed. "See, there it is. That squiggly line. That's the creek."

I glanced at the map, then leaned forward to get a better look. The old man certainly accomplished what he set out to do. Brush Creek had beauty to spare. From the sky you could see its almost perfect design. I responded the way any professional gardener would—with delight and not a small dose of envy.

"How did the nuns come to live here?" I asked.

The pilot shook his head. Funny, I'd been up with him on maybe a dozen trips and this was the first time we'd said more than a few words to one another.

"He planned to pass the estate on to his children," he said. "But some things you can't plan for, I guess. His wife died a long time before he did and his kids had no real interest in keeping the place up. So when he heard about this group of nuns who devoted themselves to taking care of poor children all over the world he decided to give his home to them, as a place for them to take a rest from their work. Only one condition: They had to keep it exactly as it was."

Neither of us said anything for a while, as if even this small exchange of local lore had been too intimate.

I broke the silence with a laugh.

"What's so funny?" the pilot asked.

"I was just thinking," I said. "This should be a breeze. Who better to ask for a Christmas tree than nuns?"

I relaxed on the way back. It was still only spring and I might just have gotten Christmas out of the way.

※ ※ ※

I drove out to the convent the next day.

I didn't mind getting out of the office. The building janitors were on strike and the place was in chaos. Now on top of everything else I had to do I was in charge of making sure everyone had trash bags. What a mess!

I've got a 22-acre operation at Rockefeller Center. We change the garden arrangement on the Promenade eleven or twelve times a year. I do the design, find the plants and am in charge of the planting, the primping and the pruning. Plus, we have 500 street trees to tend to and who knows how many indoor flowers and plants that have to be redone every two weeks.

And then there's the tree.

The guy who hired me used to take care of the tree. Now *he* was a sentimental guy. He loved doing it. Even when he got promoted he kept that part of the job. Once in a while he'd take me out with him. I thought he just wanted company. Little did I know he was grooming me to take over.

He knew I wasn't keen on it. But just before he retired he told me, "You're the gardener. You take care of the greenery around here. The tree is green. It's yours."

"Thanks," I muttered, making no attempt to hide my lack of enthusiasm.

"It'll be good for you," he said, laughing. "Soften you up a little."

"Besides," he added, "you're good at it."

I've thought about giving the tree to someone else— but the truth is, much as I complain about it, *I am* good at it.

At least it gets me outdoors. I may be a gardener, but I spend most of my time parked in front of the computer or on the telephone. So spending a pleasant spring day in the country seemed just fine to me—especially when I knew I had that tree in my sights. No dreaded dead ends in front of me this time.

It was a long drive into the prettiest part of New Jersey. The convent was set back quite a distance from the main road. The gravel drive leading to it was lined with dogwood trees in full bloom and I rolled down my window so I could bask in their scent.

Though I had seen the convent from the air, I wasn't prepared for the way it looked when I rounded the last bend. Propped up on top of a gentle slope, it had the imposing size of a castle, but the charm of a little girl's dollhouse. Mysterious tiny windows popped out of the steeply angled roof like secret peepholes, while the

downstairs windows were huge, clearly designed to make the outdoors and indoors part of each other. The building seemed to go on forever; just when it seemed my eyes had finally found the end of it, I spotted yet another wall angling off in another direction.

The nun who answered the door invited me in and then went to get Sister Frances, who ran the place. We had spoken on the phone.

As I stood in the foyer, I caught a glimpse of a large room full of beautiful paintings, comfortable furniture and luxurious carpets that looked like something out of the Arabian Nights.

I was taken aback by the swell surroundings.

"Do you like our home?" a friendly voice asked.

I looked up and saw a nun with a round pink face and amused, intelligent eyes watching me gawk. I laughed, a little embarrassed.

Sister Frances took me on a tour. Every room seemed flooded with light. "The Old Man made sure you could always look out, no matter where you sat," she explained. So even chairs whose backs were to windows faced large mirrors angled so they offered a perfectly composed view of the outdoors. The main rooms were grand; the bedrooms were cozy and all of it was deliberate. We ended up in a large parlor, sitting in front of windows that opened onto the garden and the fields beyond.

"As you have probably gathered, this is no ordinary convent," said Sister Frances. "Most of the sisters work with children all over the world, usually in places that are far away, in every possible sense. They come here to rest."

Though she moved and talked with the peppy enthusiasm of a natural organizer, I began to realize that her vigor was deceptive. Sister Frances had been around a long time.

We chatted a bit more about the convent, and about the small group of nuns who lived there all year round. I noticed that we weren't alone, though it was very quiet. There were nuns reading or talking in small groups in almost every room.

But it didn't take Sister Frances long to get down to business.

"So you're interested in one of our trees?" she said.

I told her I was and tried to describe its location as best I could.

She listened carefully, then smiled. "I thought so," she said.

She began to get up from her chair, rather cautiously. I jumped to help her, but she waved me away, laughing.

"No, no. I've gotten around this earth for seventy-some years with God's help alone and I'm too old to change my ways now."

Sister Frances made her way to the window and pointed. "Go down there and you'll see a path that will take you to your tree," she said. "But the decision isn't mine. It's Sister Anthony's."

I was heartened by her words. She did say "your tree," didn't she?

"Where can I find Sister Anthony?" I asked her.

"Just go on down to the tree," she said. "I suspect you'll find her."

Chapter Two
SISTER ANTHONY

The air was rich with the smell of spring. At first I walked with my brisk city steps, aimed toward my destination. But I slowed down to admire a fine orchard, and then, finding myself surrounded by so much beauty, began stopping every few yards.

It felt strange. Stopping. I'm always working a tight schedule—the big spring Flower Show at one end of the year, Christmas at the other and all of the ongoing plant exhibits in between.

Finally I arrived at a big stand of evergreens, just as Sister Frances said I would. My heart was beating fast, as if I was about to go on a blind date. I couldn't believe my own foolishness.

I walked through the trees into a clearing. It took my eyes a second to adjust from the shadows to the light. I blinked, and there it was! The tree I'd seen from the sky, looking exactly as I hoped it would. It had the weight of majesty, the delicacy of grace.

"Hello there!"

I jumped a little. I'd been so mesmerized by the tree I hadn't even noticed the small figure in black standing at the far side of the clearing.

She walked over briskly and stuck out her hand.

"You must be the man from Rockefeller Center," she said.

It took me a few seconds to respond. She had a surprisingly strong grip.

"Yes," I said. "Jesse King. And you are . . ."

"I'm Sister Anthony," she said.

Then she turned toward the tree.

"He's beautiful, isn't he?" she said.

"He sure is," I said.

"Well, young man," she said, "come and talk to me." She crossed over to the tree and sat down, with her habit spread around her like a tent that had collapsed.

There was something unnerving about this nun. She had the manner and the voice of a mature woman—she was well into her fifties—but the restless energy of a child. She moved faster than I did. Her face was small yet arresting, but it was her eyes that really caught me, so dark they were almost black, but very bright.

I sat down next to her feeling tongue-tied, like a kid. And while I may have seemed young to Sister Anthony, I was no kid.

Since I didn't say anything, she began for me.

"So you want Tree," she said.

"Tree?" I repeated blankly.

She laughed. "I'm sorry. It must sound strange to you, to hear an old thing like me talk that way. But I've known Tree since I was a little girl—and he was a sapling, for that matter. We grew up together."

I was feeling like Dorothy must have felt when she landed in Oz. Even weirder, I liked it there, but I still had a job to do. I put on my doing-business voice. "So, I imagine you'd be thrilled to see your tree become the most famous tree in the world."

Sister Anthony looked at me as though I was crazy. "Why?" she asked.

I began to mumble something about making millions of children all over the world feel happy, but I already knew it was over. I didn't have my Christmas tree after all. It was May and in a minute it would be December and now, instead of cruising through the summer I'd be on the road looking for a tree that couldn't possibly be as good as this one.

She must have seen the misery on my face.

"Oh, I think it must be wonderful!" she said. "It's just not the thing for Tree. He has a lot of work to do here."

Then she told me how the nuns would come to the clearing for special services, and have picnics under her tree in the summer, because his branches provided such lovely shade. She told me how she had been teaching nature classes here in the clearing to children from town for so long that some of them had even brought their grandchildren to visit Tree.

All of this emerged in one long, cheery burst of words. Finally, she stopped and looked directly into my eyes.

"I haven't told you the entire truth," she said softly. "Sister Frances told me why you were coming and said it was up to me. But there are many trees for you to choose from. I have only one Tree."

My disappointment faded after I heard the intensity in her voice. There was a depth of feeling there I could only guess at.

I stretched my legs and started to pull myself to my feet.

"I guess I should go," I said, as gently as I knew how.

"No, don't go," said Sister Anthony. "I brought lunch." She nodded at an old satchel lying on the ground. "When Sister Frances said you were a horticulturist I was hoping we might have a chance to talk. I'm considered the expert around here and it isn't easy being the one expected to have all the answers."

"You're telling me," I said, plopping right back on the ground.

She handed me a sandwich.

"So tell me," she said. "What does it mean to be the chief gardener at Rockefeller Center?"

I liked talking to her. Her knowledge was impressive. It was nice to find someone who knew the difference between an azalea and a rhododendron. But inevitably the talk turned to the Christmas tree and what a pain in the neck it was.

"It sounds like you *hate* Christmas!" she said.

I hesitated, then decided to tell the truth. It was that kind of day.

"I'm a horticulturist plain and simple. Christmas is a duty I didn't ask for."

I knew I sounded like a curmudgeon, but I was tired of putting on a happy face about it, and she seemed willing to listen.

"You start dreading Christmas. It's the pressure. I live Christmas all year round. Before one Christmas comes, I'm working on the next. What's worse, you spend so much time trying to find this great tree and then people don't even understand what they're looking at. They've gotten so used to artificial trees or real trees sheared to 'perfection' they think the individuality of a real tree is a kind of imperfection."

She looked perplexed.

"Look up there, Sister," I said. "See how your tree's branches go this way and that?"

She replied, a little defensive. "Why, that's what gives him character."

I stared at her.

"What's wrong?" she asked.

I shook my head.

"Nothing. I was just surprised to hear you use that word."

"Why?" she asked.

"Once," I said, "a reporter was interviewing me about how we get the tree and she asked, 'What makes one tree different from the other?' I tried to explain it to her. I talked about shading and triangles and density but I could see she wasn't satisfied. I was getting annoyed. I didn't have time for this. How do you explain a feeling you have for something to somebody who hasn't experienced it?"

Then Sister Anthony said gently, "Well, what did you tell her?"

"Character," I said. "I told her it's character. My Great-Aunt Margaret had it. Many women were more beautiful than she was, but none had her presence. When she walked into a room she held it."

We sat in silence for a while, eating our sandwiches.

Sister Anthony spoke, with a teasing note in her voice. "Well, perhaps you don't hate Christmas so much after all."

I was a little embarrassed at having let my guard down. I generally like to play it cool.

I shrugged. "For me it's like theater. We build the set, light the tree and pull the curtain! The show begins."

She raised her eyebrows.

"All right," I said. "It's pretty poetic if you're a visitor. Especially when it snows. The ice skaters out on the rink below the tree, the bushes, they all sparkle, like they're trying to outdo the tree. You know what I mean?"

She shook her head. "Not really."

I was incredulous.

"Haven't you ever seen the tree at Rockefeller Center? On television, at least?"

She shook her head again, smiling. "I don't venture far from Brush Creek and we don't have a television. We try to keep things quiet for our visiting nuns. They need a rest from the troubles they see in the outside world."

It was one of those times when you realize there are always limits on the kinship you may feel for someone. Sister Anthony might know a lot about nature, but what did she know of the real world? I felt like a jerk for having opened myself up to her, for thinking that she would understand.

She looked upset, as though she, too, sensed that the moment between us had been lost. Hoping to make a polite exit, I launched into my standardized riff on the tree.

"I see the tree as the crown jewel of Rockefeller Center," I was saying in a monotone, when Sister Anthony seemed to drift off to some other place.

"The city is our jewel," she murmured.

"Excuse me?" I said.

She repeated herself. "Anna, the city is our jewel."

I shook my head. "I don't understand."

When she didn't reply I reached over and tapped her on the shoulder.

Now it was her turn to look surprised. She shook her head and started to get up. "You'll have to forgive me," she said. "Something you said took me back to another time."

"Who was Anna?" I asked her.

She settled back on the grass. "I don't think she would be of much interest to you."

"Too late for that," I said. "Tell me."

Suddenly the sense of camaraderie I'd felt before returned, as quickly as it had vanished. Sister Anthony seemed as she had been, vigorous and full of humor.

"It's no great mystery," she said. "I was Anna, many many years ago."

She looked mischievous. "It may surprise you, but we nuns don't arrive on this earth wearing habits, you know. I was a little girl once. And I was born in New York City."

"Tell me more," I said.

"So you'd like to hear a story, would you? All right," she said, "I'll tell you how a girl named Anna from New York came to Brush Creek."

A change came over her then, and I realized that she was either a born storyteller or a practiced one. It came as no surprise to hear her begin with "once upon a time."

Chapter Three
ANNA

Once upon a time I was a girl named Anna, after a grandmother I never knew. I had no brothers and sisters, not even a pet, though I used to pretend the cat that yowled in the alley behind our building was mine.

My mother died when I was born and my father died not many years later, when I was five. So I had a feeling more than a memory of my parents. It was a very good feeling, from a mixture of pictures and words that came to me when I wasn't expecting them, most often in the middle of the night.

The pictures were made up of the most beautiful colors, a series of bright lights, reflected from above and below. And I would always hear the same words, spoken in Father's warm, gravelly voice: "The city is our jewel."

We had a neighbor, Mrs. Ellis, who had always been kind to me. She lived on the ground floor of our building and always kept her door open. Whenever she saw me come in she would call me over for some bread hot from the oven or to give me a piece of yarn to make something with. In the good times, when Father had work, Mrs. Ellis would watch me—or rather, I would watch her. She took in ironing from the ladies who lived in fine houses on Washington Square. I remember spending hours watching her heat the heavy black iron on the stove, then carefully return wrinkled shirts to their original crispness. She could even do lace sleeves.

When Father died I stayed with Mrs. Ellis, but one morning, not long after the funeral, she looked up from her ironing and said, "I wish I could take care of you, Anna, but I'm too old to start raising children again. Since there's no one else to tend to it, I'll have to take you there until they find your aunt."

I didn't know anything about my aunt, or where "there" was, but I was excited at the prospect of an outing, after so many days and weeks of stillness, watching Father get sicker and sicker. Though I missed him, I was too young to comprehend that I would never see him again and I thought he would be pleased for me to be out and about.

"We're great roamers, you and I," he would say to me. We used to take long walks together, sometimes all the way to Central Park from our little apartment in Greenwich Village.

I packed my few things into a bag, as Mrs. Ellis told me to, and we were about to leave when I spotted my father's old satchel hanging on a hook by the stove. After he died it became my most prized possession—it was all that I had left of him.

"Oh, wait just a minute," I asked Mrs. Ellis, who was always patient with me. "I mustn't forget my satchel for collecting things."

I heard Mrs. Ellis sniffle and mutter under her breath, " Poor little thing. All she's collected so far has been trouble."

When I asked her what she meant, Mrs. Ellis patted my face. "Nothing, dear," she said. "Nothing at all. Now let's hurry along."

I had only recently learned how to skip and as I skipped alongside Mrs. Ellis I felt happy, especially when I heard we were going to a Children's Home. Much as I'd loved Father, I didn't have any friends my age and I yearned to play games and whisper secrets like the children in the books Father used to read to me.

So when we arrived at the home and Mrs. Ellis asked me if I'd like her to stay awhile I said no. I do remember how hard she hugged me before she left and how eager I was to go inside.

Until that day, I had always been a happy child. How could I not have been with a father who used to greet every morning by peering out the window and asking: "What lies out there for us today?"

We were almost never disappointed. We always found something I had never seen before, something new and wonderful.

Unfortunately, at the Children's Home I found something I'd never experienced before—something I wish I hadn't.

Gloom.

It wasn't the darkness. Our apartment only got light in the late afternoon, when the sun moved across the sky to the west. Father had explained that to me one day when I asked how one place could be both light and dark.

Nor was I put off by the home's cavernous appearance, or the noise of so many children. I was a city child and a poor one at that. Comfort and quiet were things I'd heard about in stories, but not experienced. And the home was well-maintained, under the circumstances.

No, the gloomy feeling came from something that happened just after I arrived.

A soft-spoken lady showed me to my bed, which was the fifth in a long line of beds with their corners neatly tucked in. "You can put your things away and then get to know the other girls," said the lady, who seemed to be in a great hurry. At the time I took her briskness for coldness. In retrospect I realize the poor thing must have been overworked. There simply weren't enough adults to take care of all the children.

I placed my bag and satchel underneath the bed and

waited. Soon a girl with pretty dark hair came along. She was much taller than I was and seemed older, but I had always been small for my age. Father used to call me Sparrow.

"Hello!" I said, probably too brightly. I think I just assumed that she would be glad to see me. I had always been surrounded by loving people.

"What's in the funny bag with the straps?"

That's how she introduced herself. I learned later that her name was Doreen.

I held out my hand like Father had taught me. "My name is Anna," I said.

"Is that what I asked you?" she replied in an angry voice.

Though I suppose it should have been obvious, I still didn't understand that she didn't want to be friends. I opened my satchel and gently spilled out my precious collection onto the bed. It had belonged to my father and was made up of twigs and leaves and nuts from trees, and pieces of bark. There were also four neatly folded pieces of paper with drawings of the various parts of trees. They were labeled across the top, in my father's careful handwriting: Sycamore. Maple.

Gingko. Oak. While Doreen watched, I made little piles on each piece of paper. The sycamore leaves, twigs, nuts and bark went on the sycamore drawing, the oak on the oak, and so on.

"There," I said proudly when I was finished.

Doreen leaned over the bed as though examining the things I'd laid out. Then, to my horror, she grabbed the oak pile, broke the twigs, crumbled the leaves into pieces and threw the bark on the floor, crushing it with her heavy shoe. Only the little acorn escaped by rolling under the bed.

"What a ninny you are," she sneered and put up her fists, as if waiting for me to try and hit her.

I felt my face burning. I was so angry. But Father had always said anger doesn't cure anything, and I knew it would hurt him to disobey.

So I didn't say a word to Doreen. I just gathered up my twigs and papers, knelt down and swept the crushed pieces of bark into my hand, and gently laid them all back into my satchel.

From then on, I was known by the adults at the home as The Quiet One. I did what I was told, nothing more and nothing less. The women who took care of us were really quite nice. At first they tried to coax me to speak out, to play. But there were so many children to take care of that it was easy for them to forget about me because I wasn't any trouble at all.

As for the other children, they left me alone. The kind ones, I imagine, had their own troubles to occupy them; the bullies like Doreen ignored me once they found I wouldn't rise to their taunts. I simply waited for the day when I could once again look out of the window and not be afraid to ask: "What lies out there for me today?"

❋ ❋ ❋

Then early one day, just after dawn, before the morning bell had rung, I woke up to find myself staring up at two very tall people. Maybe they weren't really that tall, they just seemed so to me. I was six by then. I will never forget the date. It was April 2, 1935, almost a year to the day since I had said good-bye to Mrs. Ellis.

The man and the woman introduced themselves, but I was so sleepy I couldn't make out what they said, just that they had been sent by somebody to pick me up.

I heard the woman say, "Come on, dear, get dressed and pack your things. You're coming with us."

For a minute I shivered I was so excited, until I remembered the last time a kind lady had taken me somewhere. I didn't object, however. But then, I wouldn't have. My objective was not to be noticed, and I managed by doing what I was told.

It took only a minute for me to get ready. I left with what I had brought. I hadn't grown very much, so everything still fit except my shoes, which had been passed along to an even smaller girl. I pulled my satchel out from under my pillow, where it had remained, unopened since the day I'd arrived, and I was ready to leave.

"What a marvelous satchel, Anna," the lady said. "Look at all those straps and buckles! What's inside?"

I was too frightened to reply—or to even look at her. I shuffled along with my eyes on the ground.

The woman whispered something to the man. I couldn't hear what she said, but when I sneaked a glance upward, I saw that she seemed worried about me. I would have liked to answer her; I could sense that she was a kind person. But I wasn't ready to take a chance like that.

I didn't pay much attention to what the grown-ups were chatting about as we walked along. I was too caught up in the moment, of once again experiencing that familiar, happy sensation of being out on the street.

When we arrived at their automobile and the man opened the door, it took me a minute to realize I was supposed to go inside. I had never been inside an automobile before!

I scrambled in and watched with excitement as the man put the key in the ignition and then felt the engine start, with a loud roar and a bump. I wanted to laugh out loud, but I had just spent a year learning to keep my feelings locked inside. Those poor people! They must have thought I was miserable, sitting up so straight in my seat not saying a thing, except *please* and *thank you* when I was given something to eat and drink.

We drove for quite a while, long enough for the scenery flashing by the window to turn from gray to green. This new world seemed vast and a little lonely to me. We went for miles without seeing a person, only a cow here and there. The beauty of the scenery only made me feel increasingly scared and sad as I realized I now had nothing to connect me to my old life in New York, not even concrete.

We turned off the main road onto another road before we finally rounded the bend that led to the most amazing building I'd ever seen. So many fanciful windows and nooks, it looked like something from a picturebook. It was Brush Creek, of course.

I was overcome with the strangest feeling. My parents had sent for me—they had been waiting for me in this wonderful new home, together with the cat from the alley. Maybe Mrs. Ellis was here, too. There certainly was plenty of room for everyone.

I pulled on the car door handle, trying to open it. All of a sudden I didn't care if my happiness showed.

"There you go," said the man, reaching back and pushing the door for me.

I jumped out of the car and found myself skipping across the lawn. I thought I'd forgotten how.

I began to yell, "Hello! Hello! I'm here!"

The door to the giant house opened and someone came out, a big smile on her face.

I stopped and remained absolutely still as I realized what a terrible mistake I had made.

The person walking toward me was a woman, but she looked very odd, all tucked into a flowing black robe as if she was trying to hide. I had never seen a nun before.

My heart sank and I felt like crying. Of course my parents weren't here. Only more strangeness.

"You must be Anna," said the cloaked woman. "Welcome to Brush Creek." She had plump, rosy cheeks and little round eyeglasses. It was hard to tell if she was old or young.

I turned and looked for an explanation from the people who had brought me here.

"Anna, why do you look so shocked?" the woman said. "We told you you'd be coming here to stay with the Sisters, who have so kindly agreed to take care of you."

Then I did remember hearing something about "sisters" while we were walking to the car, but since I didn't have any sisters I had assumed they weren't talking to me and had stopped listening.

The nun with the rosy cheeks was Sister Frances, who took charge then as she does now. "My name is Sister Frances," she said. "Why don't you come in and let me show you around."

What choice did I have? I picked up my little bag and my satchel and went inside.

❅ ❅ ❅

Sister Anthony stopped talking, abruptly. "My good-ness," she said. "Look at the time. I can't believe I've rattled on like this."

We'd been sitting there a long while. There was so much I wanted to ask her, so much I wanted to tell her, too, but I could see our time was up. So I thanked her for an interesting afternoon, and went on my way, surprised at how reluctant I was to leave.

Chapter Four
FRIENDS

 I didn't expect to see Sister Anthony again after that strange afternoon of companionship and revelation. Certainly I had no plans to ask about her tree again. I make it a rule never to interfere with the relationship between owners and their trees, no matter how tempting it is.

Many times, though, I felt the urge to talk to her. I didn't understand what it was, exactly, that drew me to her. I had plenty of people to talk plants with, and her cloistered life didn't seem to have anything in common with mine. Though I grew up in the country in Ohio, I've become a happy city boy. I may complain, like everyone else, about the noise and the inconvenience and the dirt, but I also love the possibility in it all. New York suits someone like me, who's congenitally unsettled. Orphans and nuns were not on my agenda.

I decided the connection I felt with Sister Anthony that day was born of fatigue and frustration. I'd just been working too hard. Brush Creek, indeed!

Then she called. It must have been early autumn. I can't place the date exactly. I only remember I had already found a Christmas tree for that year. I didn't need anything from her.

She was teaching a nature class and wanted to know if I would come and tell the children about how I find the Rockefeller Christmas tree. She was friendly on the phone, though slightly formal.

I could have made up an excuse. I usually do. But something, I didn't know what, made me say yes.

❄ ❄ ❄

I found her in the clearing, surrounded by a group of young children, who were maybe eight or nine years old. I stood at the edge and watched as she handed them pieces of colored paper.

"You're the Sycamore group," she was saying to the children holding red sheets, when she noticed me.

"Hello," she said, waving me over. Her cheeks were bright from the nip in the air. "Let me finish up with this and I'll turn them over to you. Do you have some time? If you don't, I can do this later."

I told her to go ahead. I had nothing else planned for the afternoon.

She had divided the class into kinds of trees, grouped by the color of the paper they'd been given. On each sheet she'd drawn a likeness of the bark, the fruit or seed, the twig and the leaf of each kind of tree. The children were supposed to find examples and bring them the next time they met.

I felt nervous as I watched their enthusiasm. This was a tough act to follow. Yet during my little presentation they listened closely and asked questions that seemed to spring from real curiosity. I had spoken to enough school groups to know that these kids had been in the hands of a gifted teacher.

When I was finished, they still weren't ready to leave.

"Tell us a story," one of them called out.

Sister Anthony smiled, then with a look of mock seriousness stared up at the sky.

"Let me see," she said, "where is the sun? Do we have enough time?"

It seemed that this storytelling time was a ritual that concluded all of Sister Anthony's nature classes, since before she had a chance to finish asking her question the children were looking upward with the same mock seriousness and yelling: "Yes!"

"All right," said Sister Anthony, then she paused.

"Would you like to hear about how I came to meet Tree?"

There were more shouts of "yes." But before she began, she thanked me for coming and told me I didn't have to stay. "No, no, I'd like to hear this," I said, despite the image of piles of unanswered telephone messages that flashed through my brain. I needed to find out what it was that had pulled me back there.

From the start, I could see the kids were willing to go wherever her story would take them. And so was I.

❄ ❄ ❄

Many years ago, a little girl came to Brush Creek to live. She was all alone in the world, and her name was Anna. I was that girl.

I had arrived after a long journey. Sister Frances—yes, she was here even then—led me up two flights of narrow stairs to my room, which was way up under the eaves. It was a tiny room, with a very big window right next to the bed. There was also a little bureau and a chair and a closet. It seemed very grand to me. I'd never had my own room before.

I remember Sister Frances saying, "You will say your prayers before you go to sleep, won't you?"

I nodded, but I wasn't sure I could live up to my end of the bargain. It's probably hard for you children to imagine, but I was quite out of the practice of saying my prayers. I'd been living in an orphanage for about a year and had forgotten how. I remember putting on my nightgown and hanging my satchel on a hook in the closet before crawling into bed. I tried to remember the bedtime prayer I used to say with my father, but I couldn't. Finally I simply said *thank you for letting me be in this beautiful place*, then turned over so I could look out of the window. In the black sky I saw tiny dots of light, so many I couldn't begin to count them. I didn't know what they were! As I fell asleep I told myself to ask Sister Frances in the morning.

My face was warm when I woke up. The sun was pouring in through the window.

I quickly dressed and went downstairs to find Sister Frances. No one was in the kitchen or anywhere in the house. I had no idea where everybody had gone and I was a little bit frightened.

I didn't know what to do, so I went into the big sitting room in the center of the house and just stood quietly and waited. Off in the distance I heard a lovely, silvery sound. I wanted to go outside and see what it was, but I was too afraid.

At last I saw a large group of nuns walking through the garden, coming toward the house. They'd been at morning prayer, though I didn't know it at the time. Brush Creek and its routines were completely new to me.

"Ah, you're awake," said Sister Frances when she saw me. She told me where everyone had been and asked me if I was hungry, which I was. I was still feeling a little shy though, so without saying a word I followed the nuns into the dining hall, just beyond the kitchen. Oh, that breakfast tasted so delicious, though it was just a bowl of oatmeal. I must have gotten a strong appetite from the fresh air that had filled my room the night before.

The food gave me the courage to walk right up to Sister Frances after breakfast. "Could you tell me something?" I asked her.

Later, Sister Frances would tell me she was delighted to see me speak so boldly. She wasn't sure how I would adjust to my new home. As you all know, the visiting nuns at Brush Creek work with children, but I was the first child to actually live at the convent. It was slightly unusual, but times were different then. It had all been arranged by my aunt, my only surviving relative. She herself was a nun who lived very far away, but she had once spent time on retreat at Brush Creek.

But to get back to my story.

Sister Frances told me she would try to answer my question.

"What are those little dots outside my window?" I asked.

By then we had been joined by Sister Lucia, who didn't have much patience, I'm afraid.

"What do you mean, little dots?" she said.

I don't think Sister Lucia meant to sound as sharp as she did, but she scared me nevertheless. I replied, "Up in the sky."

Sister Frances must have seen how frightened I was. She knelt down so her eyes were level with mine, as if to comfort me.

"Those are stars, Anna. Of course you didn't see many in New York City."

Her warmth encouraged me to speak right up again. "Oh, yes, I did," I said. "When I was very small, I saw a star in New York, but it was much brighter and bigger than any of the ones I saw last night."

"Ridiculous," snapped Sister Lucia. "The child must have been dreaming. Go into the kitchen and see if you can be of some help."

I looked up at Sister Frances for guidance. "Run along, Anna," she said in a gentle voice.

I obeyed, feeling terribly sad that even here, in this beautiful place, I was made to feel so apart and alone— it was just like being at the Children's Home. Without thinking, I slipped out the kitchen door and began to run. I didn't know where I was going, I just wanted to be by myself.

The grass was wet. It was still early and the morning dew hadn't had a chance to dry in the sun. My feet were getting soaked, but I barely noticed.

I ran up the slope behind the convent, past the hedges and the large square of earth that had been plowed for that year's vegetable garden. I ran past the apple orchard, where the trees were just beginning to bud with little bursts of light green.

My breath began to come in gasps but I kept running, right through a stand of tall evergreen trees until I came to a clearing on the other side. At first I was too winded to cry. All I wanted to do was rest. I flung myself to the ground and found myself staring up at a big fat cloud that had just drifted over my head. Then, strangely, I no longer felt like crying at all. I was very calm, though I still felt lonely. I couldn't bear the thought of going back to that big house, which now didn't seem beautiful at all.

After the cloud passed, I sat up and for the first time since I had run out of the house really noticed my surroundings. I was here—in this clearing, which was surrounded by grand trees, just as it is now. It seemed very cozy to me, like a private nook just for me. Except for the sound of birds cawing and twittering, I was alone.

And yet I felt as though someone was watching me. I looked all over but didn't see anyone. Then my eye caught sight of something on the other side of the clearing—something small. I walked over and couldn't help but laugh.

Can you guess what it was?

It was a perfect little tree, a miniature version of the huge evergreens standing at the edge of the clearing. It was just about my size!

"Oh, you are so beautiful," I said, right out loud. "Can I touch you?"

I couldn't say for certain, but it seemed to me as though the tree's branches rippled ever so slightly.

Though I knew how scary strangers could be, I couldn't resist. Very carefully I reached out and patted the little tree's needles. I interpreted the fact that they were ticklish to my touch as a sign of friendliness.

Then without thinking about it I began to tell the tree things I had told no one else. How much I missed my mother and father. About Sister Lucia and Sister Frances and about how lonely I felt.

I talked for quite awhile. And when I stopped I sat down next to the tree. We stayed together contentedly, warming ourselves in the sun—and somehow I felt much better.

❄ ❄ ❄

Later, when I went back to the convent that first day, it was almost lunchtime. The nuns were upset and each let me know it in her own way.

"Where have you been?" snapped Sister Lucia, ignoring Sister Frances's warning look.

"Sister Lucia is only trying to tell you we've been worried," said Sister Frances.

"Please don't worry," was all I told them. I wasn't trying to hide anything from them, but I was afraid Sister Lucia would laugh at me if I told her about Tree. Funny, that's what I called him right from the start. Simply Tree, as though there were no others.

Luckily the lunch bell rang and the empty dining room suddenly filled with nuns. My disappearance was forgotten.

After lunch, I ran up the stairs to my room and went right to my closet to get my satchel. I ran down so fast I almost knocked over one of the sisters, who was carrying a big load of dishes over to the sink.

"Slow down, child," she said to me.

I had to force myself to walk to the door. The instant I crossed the threshold, though, I began to run, leaping across the grass, which by then was dry and springy. When I reached the clearing I made myself slow down. I didn't want to alarm my new friend. I understood that he probably wasn't used to noisy little girls. The only sound was a faint *check check check* coming from somewhere above my head. Squinting against the sunlight, I peered into the thick green needles of the surrounding evergreens.

Ah-hah! Something was moving. Then I saw it. A quick little bird with bright yellow patches on the top of his head, on his breast and on his wings. *Check check check.*

This place was full of surprises. It still is.

I walked over to the tree on tiptoe.

"I have something very wonderful to show you, Tree," I said.

With great care I opened my satchel and brought out the envelopes that contained my precious collection of leaves and bark and twigs and seeds, much like the ones we've been collecting today. I spread this treasure on the grass in front of the tree and spoke to him very seriously, as though I were an adult and he were a child. "Tree," I said, "pay attention."

Naturally Tree stood quite still, but I waited a little, just to make sure he was ready.

"These leaves and things are from your cousins," I told him. I giggled quite a bit, not because I thought what I was saying was silly but because I was nervous. But the bird with the yellow patches was singing cheerfully, as though he were encouraging me to go on.

So I did. It wasn't easy, because my father had explained it all to me and he had died a long time ago. But I kept at it and remembered quite a bit of the basics. I told Tree about how to identify the various parts of trees—about bark and seeds— and showed him the difference between an oak and a sycamore. It wasn't a bad lecture for a beginner I must say, and I became quite demonstrative. "The twigs hold the leaves on, just like my arm holds my hand," I said to him, and waved my arms in the air. And I felt quite triumphant when I remembered that the leaves had something to do with providing food for the trees, though I had no idea how, exactly.

I tried looking closely at Tree, thinking I might learn something by studying his leaves. But when I got close,

I saw that he didn't have leaves like other leaves. Close up, I could see that his feathery arms were made of lots of short skinny green spikes that spiraled up along the twig. Here and there I could see a space where it looked as though one of the green spikes had fallen out. Getting as close as I could, I saw something that looked almost like a little hook where the green spike must have been.

It was all very interesting but didn't tell me a thing about how leaves made food, which was frustrating.

"You must be tired," I said to Tree, meaning, of course, that I was feeling a little tired myself. "Why don't you take a little rest. I'll lie down next to you to help you go to sleep."

Then, once again, I heard that familiar *check check check*, which reminded me to put away my seeds and things before a bird decided to disturb them.

Once everything was safely in my satchel I lay down on the grass and took a much-needed rest with my new friend Tree.

❅ ❅ ❅

By the time Sister Anthony's story was finished, the sun was well on its way to the horizon. The clearing was especially lovely as the golden light of late afternoon filtered through the needles of the evergreen trees. The children murmured their good-byes, as if they were still in the thrall of the story they'd just heard. And I think I was a little in awe myself as I shook Sister Anthony's hand. As I walked away I was struck by how sharp my hearing seemed, as though somebody had turned the volume up. Suddenly the woods seemed full of sounds I hadn't heard for twenty years. When had I stopped listening?

Chapter Five

TEACHERS

 $\mathcal{A}$nyone who has had a friend or been one knows that it takes an awful lot of work. That's especially true when one of you is human and the other is a tree. You can't exactly ask what will make your friend happy, or what's making him sad. Conversation becomes a rather imaginative game, and Sister Anthony had clearly become a master of it. (In fact, a lot of human-to-human friendships might improve if they took the care she took to understand that tree.)

This became obvious to me over the years as my Christmas-tree talk developed into an annual event. This did not feel like an obligation, because I always left with more than I came with. Though she had never left Brush Creek, Sister Anthony had an enviable excitement about life—not to mention an endless supply of stories. There was always a new crop of kids, so she could easily have repeated herself, but she continually seemed to find new mysteries to explore in the natural world, and new parables that could be drawn from her life. I don't know how she did it. I'd traveled all over the world, seen my work written up regularly in the *Times*, yet so often I felt weary of it all.

I'd like to say I sat at her feet and soaked up all that inspiration. Mostly, though, after the kids left, I'd start to complain—about the bureaucracy at work, about the public's failure to appreciate all the beauty we spread out for them at Rockefeller Center, or whatever else was driving me crazy on that particular day. Sometimes I'd have a problem I couldn't work out and Sister Anthony was almost always able to help just by asking the questions that would lead me to the answer.

"How do you do it?" I asked her one day.

"What's that?" she replied.

"Tell stories the way you do," I said, then corrected myself. "No, not only that. How did you become a teacher?"

She had been showing me a new herb garden she had planted that year. Each section was carefully marked with a tag explaining what the herb was used for, and a bit of folklore about it. I had just rubbed some rosemary between my fingers, and knew from then on the smell of rosemary would always remind me of Brush Creek.

She took some time to answer. "It all started with Tree, I suppose. After we first met he became part of my routine. I would go to morning prayers with the Sisters and help clean up after breakfast and then on sunny days I would immediately head outdoors."

Unconsciously, her face tilted toward the sun. "Every day I discovered something new—a bird whose song I hadn't heard before, a patch of wildflowers. My expeditions always ended with Tree, so I could report on what I'd found that day. No matter how much fun I had on my own, my adventures always felt the truest when I turned them into stories for Tree."

I wanted to know more. "I understand that," I said, "but you've acquired a pretty impressive body of knowledge. Tree may have gotten you started but how did you know what stories to tell? Did you learn it all by yourself."

"Oh no," she said. "I had wonderful teachers."

I was surprised. "Where did you go to school?" I asked.

She laughed. "Right here," she said. "Remember, I grew up in a different era. No one paid much attention to whether you were formally enrolled in school or not. I would say that my schooling was unusual but very complete.

"Let's see now, there was Sister Matilda, who was excellent at math, who taught me my numbers. Sister Stephen taught me history, with lots of attention to the great battles. I also have her to thank for my chess game.

"Then there was Sister Agnes, who introduced me to science. She did most of the cooking and let me use her kitchen as a laboratory. I learned geography from the visiting nuns. They would take me into the library and point to where they'd been on the globe, and tell me what life was like there. All of them took turns with reading and writing. They all had favorite stories they wanted to pass on to someone and I suppose I was the someone they had at hand."

I interrupted. "So who was your favorite?"

"This probably won't surprise you," she said. "I met her through Tree." And with that, she began yet another story.

❄ ❄ ❄

I was frustrated because I knew I hadn't yet found a way to speak Tree's language, I didn't know what would really interest him. I felt that he would trust me only if I could tell him about the world, just as my father had done for me. I had already figured out who could help me, I just didn't know how to persuade her.

Her name was Sister Mary and she was the gardener at Brush Creek. I knew it wasn't going to be easy. While the other nuns went out of their way to chat with me, Sister Mary kept to herself. Whatever you asked her, whether it was if she'd like more tea or what time it was, her answer was always the same: "Hmmmm." She was usually outside, either working or wandering around talking to herself.

She was also a bit of a mess. She always had a smudge of dirt on her forehead, and strands of hair kept popping out from under her veil, no matter how often she tucked them in. I had noticed something else. Whenever the faintest sound came from the sky, Sister Mary would automatically say the name of the bird, then begin pointing upward, all the while rotating like a human telescope. The other nuns used to say, "Sister Mary's a little distracted." But she kept the flowers and bushes beautifully tended and everyone agreed her tomatoes were the best they'd ever tasted.

She was eccentric and would have seemed frightening except for one thing. She had the most engaging eyes I had ever seen. They were deep blue and crinkly at the edges. They were smiling eyes.

I began to secretly follow Sister Mary wherever she went. When she wasn't outdoors, she was studying in the library, always in the same section, where the books about plants and birds were.

As soon as she left, I would retrieve the book she'd been reading and open it. Most of the words were too difficult for me, so I looked at the pictures. They were lovely, but I wanted to know more.

One day I was sitting on the floor staring at one of these drawings when I felt a hand on my shoulder. I jumped straight up in the air. I hadn't heard a footstep!

Then I looked up and saw Sister Mary looking at me.

"Why have you been following me around?" she asked.

I was so surprised I couldn't speak. Sister Mary sounded . . . normal.

She didn't wait for an answer. "Let me show you something," she said, walking over to the corner of the library where there were some books in a glass case I'd never noticed. She opened the door and motioned for me to join her.

I didn't see anything special. Just a row of slender books bound in what looked like heavy brown paper.

Sister Mary pulled one of the books out. Someone had pasted a square of paper onto the front and written the title in neat letters.

"The Uninvited Guest," read Sister Mary.

She opened the book and showed me the first page. There was a little pencil drawing of a kitchen sink filled with dishes and a tiny splotch of gray. I thought it was charming.

Sister Mary read. "First, a gray shadow."

On the next page a bright green foot and tail appeared at the edge of the sink.

"Then a foot and a tail," said Sister Mary, continuing to read. Finally an entire green lizard made his appearance. He was a sleek little fellow, who seemed to dance off the page. In the story, he played, had a snack and then decided to stay.

When the story was finished I laughed and clapped and wanted to see the rest of these funny little books—

Never Underestimate the Cunning of a Fly and *How the Sour Apple Tree Learned to Smile,* are two I remember.

I asked where they had come from. They seemed so perfect for children.

"The old man who built this place made them for his children," Sister Mary told me.

I remember her sighing and looking a bit sad. "It's a shame none of them chose to take these books with them," she said.

When I asked Sister Mary to read me the book about the fly she replied, "No, you read to me." She helped me make out the words I didn't recognize, and was wonderful about answering all my questions about flies and lizards and goodness knows what else. It wasn't just reading that she taught me, but about all of the mysteries in everyday things.

❄ ❄ ❄

We had a long talk that day and when we were finished I of course ran straight to Tree.

"Listen to this, Tree," I said, "I've been telling you all kinds of things but you haven't said much about yourself to me at all. I thought maybe you were afraid or shy. But I've asked Sister Mary to help us."

I went on and on, about how Sister Mary wasn't strange at all once you got to know her and how she knew everything there was to know about trees and birds and plants, and about how grand the library was. I told him that Sister Mary even told me that one day I would be able to read all those books, which seemed impossible to me at the time.

Then I remembered. I had come to tell Tree his story.

"You are a Norway spruce," I said rather grandly, in the kind of voice you might use to tell a frog that he is really a prince. "You are one of them"—I nodded toward the tall trees at the edge of the clearing—"and they didn't come here by accident. They didn't come from seeds that were carried here by birds or the wind or . . ."

I couldn't remember if Sister Mary had told me anything else about how seeds could be carried.

"No matter," I continued. "The Old Man who used to own this place planted those big trees a long time ago. Maybe thirty or forty years."

I paused to let Tree absorb the full importance of what I was telling him. I was really quite theatrical.

"Norway spruces grow very fast and are very beautiful. They were perfect because the Old Man wanted everything to look just so right away. And then the Sisters moved here and sometime last year Sister Mary noticed a tiny little tree growing here, off on its own.

"That was you!" I shouted.

Suddenly there was much activity overhead. There was a flurry of flapping and trilling, as the birds living in the Norway spruces came out to see who was making all the racket.

I saw the familiar little birds with the yellow markings. There were others, too. Birds with red chests and other birds that were red all over. There were striped birds and plain brown ones. Birds that sang up the scale and birds that sang down. I wanted to memorize the way they looked so I could ask Sister Mary about them.

With my head tilted back so I could see the birds, I ran round and round in circles, trying to get a closer look. Finally I was so dizzy I plopped down on the ground, and rolled in the grass until I landed right next to Tree.

How lovely it was!

Then I remembered I hadn't told Tree nearly everything I had to tell him.

"Did you know?" I asked him mysteriously, "that you can make music?

"Norway spruces are used to make violins," I explained, scratching away on an imaginary violin. I was a fairly literal-minded child, so the idea of this kind of radical transformation had astounded me when Sister Mary told me about it. After that, I wanted to know all the possible uses for trees.

I told Tree how trees became paper, and paper became books. Then, having saved the best for last, I told him another use for Norway spruces. I remember I was very dramatic about it, whispering, as if this piece of information was too precious to discuss in an ordinary voice.

"Christmas trees."

I pointed to the large trees all around us, with their perfect triangles and big fancy cones. "Look at them. It's true. Norway spruces make the loveliest Christmas trees!"

Just then, the breeze picked up, ruffling Tree's branches, as though he were telling me he thought this was a very exciting proposition.

I reached over and touched his needles. "Not you, silly. You're much too small," I said to him. "Besides, you're to stay right here with me."

❄ ❄ ❄

As she finished the story, Sister Anthony squinted and wiped her eyes. "Pollen," she muttered, though I suspected it was something else.

I felt a little uncomfortable, wondering if that last bit had been aimed at me, even though I had mentally crossed her tree off my list long ago.

Still, I felt the urge to change the subject, so I asked her something I'd been wanting to know for some time.

"Sister Anthony, I have a silly question," I began.

She said something I'd heard her say many times to the children. "There are no silly questions," she said. "What is it?"

"How did you come to be called Sister Anthony?" I asked.

She laughed. "That's a very good question," she said.

"Do you see this old satchel?" She held up the worn bag she always carried everywhere. "The answer is in here."

"Okay," I said. "You've got me again. Tell me."

"Sometimes I feel as if this old satchel's become part of me, like an extra arm or leg. Over the years I've used it for all kinds of things. Sometimes to carry lunch, but mainly I like to have it with me in case I come across any unusual plants or insects."

❄ ❄ ❄

As a child I would bring my treasures back to the convent library and spread them out on an old piece of carpet that Sister Mary had given me for just that purpose. That way, I could have them in front of me while I looked them up in books, without getting anything dirty. Then when I had identified my latest collection I would reload my satchel and take what I had found out to show Tree.

One morning, however, I went to take my satchel off the hook where I always kept it and the hook was empty.

I searched everywhere—under every piece of furniture, inside every cabinet. I wandered all over the grounds, all the way to the main road, through the orchards, everywhere.

Nothing.

I was miserable. By then that satchel had traveled far with me. I had the feeling that without it I might not have become friends with Tree—it was showing him the treasures I carried in the satchel that first made me feel at home with him. Probably most important, it was the only physical thing I had left from my past.

For days I searched, inside and out.

Late one morning Sister Frances found me sitting on the back step leading into the kitchen.

"Have you looked everywhere?" she asked.

I nodded miserably, staring at the ground.

"You might try asking Saint Anthony to help you," she said.

I looked up. "Who is he?"

"He was a very kind man who lived long ago, and

who had a special gift for helping people find things. Say a little prayer and maybe he can help you," said Sister Frances.

I did as she advised. I prayed very hard—in chapel with the nuns, then again, standing next to Tree. And I thought very hard as well, trying to remember the last time I'd felt the weight of my satchel on my shoulder. But even with all my praying and concentrating I just couldn't find it.

The loss discouraged me so much that not even Tree could comfort me. One afternoon, after our daily visit, I felt too low to follow my usual route back to the convent. Instead I turned down a winding path that led to the creek—a path I'd discovered only a short time before.

I was walking along listening to the twigs crackling under my feet when suddenly I saw something brown beneath a patch of ferns. My heart started beating fast.

"Please, please, please," I said, closing my eyes. "If it's my satchel I'll never forget you, Saint Anthony."

I brushed aside the ferns. There it was, my funny satchel with its many straps and buckles. Nothing had ever seemed so beautiful to me as that little leather bag. I must have lost it the day I'd discovered the path to the creek—and then completely forgotten I'd been down there.

I kept my word. I never forgot Saint Anthony. On the day I decided to become a nun, I took his name, hoping that maybe someday I could help somebody find something important the way he had helped me.

Chapter Six
THE BLIZZARD

It was the kind of storm that would make history. Children would grow up and tell their children and their children's children where they were when the blizzard hit. No one would ever forget the night the wind howled like wild prairie dogs gone mad and sent families running for their cellars if they had them, or left them quaking under their covers if they didn't.

It was the night the world turned white. The air was so thick with snow you couldn't see your hand in front of your face if you were foolhardy enough to go out, and when the wind finally stopped, the drifts were piled so high it looked as if new mountain ranges had sprung up overnight.

I was out of the country at the time, on a much-needed vacation after the Christmas rush, checking out the plant life in Mexico so I could call it a work trip. But I heard about it later—in excruciating detail—from everyone I knew. The only reports that really interested me, though, were the ones that came from Brush Creek, first from Sister Frances, then from Sister Anthony. This is what I pieced together.

❄ ❄ ❄

Apparently, the nuns spent most of that night in prayer—for travelers on the road, for the people living in homes without enough heat and for all the animals who might not find places to hide from the storm. Sister Anthony said a special prayer for Tree. She was sick with fear for him. She was well aware of the life span of a Norway spruce, and Tree was testing the limits, even though his branches had remained thick and strong long past the time they might have started snapping and fraying.

When she finally went to sleep that night she told herself she would go out to see Tree in the morning, as soon as the wind died down. But she couldn't go to see Tree the next day. In fact, for three whole days the nuns were trapped inside the convent by giant icicles that had formed during the storm. Somehow the heat from the house had melted the snow on the roof just enough to send it dripping down the sides, where it had frozen once again into enormous icicles. None of them had ever seen anything like it. It wasn't just the size of the icicles that was startling, it was their shape. They were curved, like the sides of a harp.

They were beautiful. The few nuns who were staying at the convent when the storm hit all gathered around the big windows after breakfast and stared in silence.

"Perhaps they are a sign from God, like the dove after the flood," said one of the nuns.

"That may be," said Sister Frances. "But whatever they are they're keeping us right here. It could be dangerous to try and knock them down. Probably bring a sheet of ice down on our heads."

Sister Anthony spent many hours over the next couple of days staring out of the windows. She couldn't rest until she found out what had happened to Tree. Was he still standing?

Three days after the blizzard she was awakened by a loud crash. Then another, and another. She looked out of the window and saw big indentations in the snow below, and shards of glistening ice. The icicles had fallen.

That afternoon, dressed as warmly as possible, she set out. The peaceful walk that she had taken almost every day of her life, no matter what the weather, now seemed like a difficult journey.

It wasn't just the snow, which was two feet deep in the shallowest places, but seeing the full extent of the blizzard's fury. The peacefulness of the thick white covering it had left behind was deceptive. Much had been destroyed and the carnage was terrible. Bushes had been uprooted and the pathways were littered with broken branches and great pieces of bark. Worst of all were the roots dangling in the air from the trunks of the giant trees that had been brought down by the wind.

It was eerily still, as if every living thing had been buried under the snow. The hills that had always been so full of life now seemed more like a frozen graveyard.

Eventually, Sister Anthony reached the stand of trees that led to the clearing. Her heart lifted when she saw that most of them were still upright, but then she remembered Tree didn't have the protection of other trees. He stood alone, completely vulnerable to the storm.

She pushed on, walking as firmly as she could through the snow. Finally, she stood at the edge of the clearing and with a small cry sank to her knees.

There was Tree, his vast snow-covered branches waving gently, as if it were a spring afternoon and everything was the same as it had always been.

Sister Anthony picked herself up and went over to her friend. She laid her cheek against his bark. He felt strong as ever, and warm against her icy face.

Cold as she was, she stayed there a long time, as though to assure Tree that she would always be by his side. Finally she turned and was walking slowly toward the convent when she was overcome by the sensation that Tree was gone. She made her way back as fast as the snow allowed, struggling for the second time that day up the slope that led to the clearing. But there was Tree, proud and tall against the fading light.

❅ ❅ ❅

Still, the awful feeling that Tree had been damaged somehow by the storm wouldn't go away. She began to worry more and more about Tree's health. After a severe winter a tree could look healthy for a while, but it might well be vulnerable to being toppled, like the big trees that had fallen that winter. In fact, one more harsh winter might do Tree in.

After all, no matter how well he looked, he was very old for a Norway spruce.

Day after day she visited Tree, studying him from every angle. He looked so strong and powerful, she couldn't imagine that he could be weak inside. But she couldn't ignore all the trees lying on the ground, trees that had seemed invulnerable before the storm that were now split open, splintered into pieces. She knew she couldn't stand to see her friend come to such an end.

Spring came. The earth thawed, the grounds were cleared of the sad remains of the storm and once again the children began meeting with Sister Anthony in the clearing next to Tree.

❄ ❄ ❄

That's when I got the call. She was casual, asking if I'd like to come up for the day—but I knew there was more to it than that.

I sat with the children in a circle and listened as she began to talk quietly.

"I was thinking about something I wanted to tell you—about the first time I realized that both Tree and I had grown up. He had shot up past me a number of years before and his branches were wonderfully thick and strong. Now the red crossbills hung upside down on his branches and pecked at his cones and he offered shelter to many birds—robins, sparrows, purple finches, chickadees, and of course the myrtle warblers, the birds with the yellow markings who first greeted me with their *check check check* when Tree and I first met. Tree welcomed them all."

As she spoke, she was accompanied by various trillings and warblings, as if the birds were responding to a roll call. Although she was looking directly at the children, she seemed very far away.

"I remember our conversation very well. I was leaning against his trunk, telling him how Sister Frances kept urging me to think about going out into the world, about maybe becoming a horticulturist or a teacher. I knew she wanted what was best for me but I also knew what would make me happy.

"I knew that I loved it here, listening to the birds calling one another and to the sound of the wind tickling the tops of the trees, loved watching the changing colors of the landscape, the hills going from green to brown to gray, then to green again. And where would I ever hear anything as beautiful as the Sisters singing at vespers?

"I'd read so many stories about people searching for faith, for a reason to live and I'd found that right here," continued Sister Anthony. "Every day I wake up and look out my window and I feel excited. I've never stopped asking: 'What lies out there for me today?'"

She smiled at the children, full of warmth and tenderness. "I've found all of you here. It's been such a wonderful thing for me to watch you learn and grow."

She paused, remembering her story.

"I curled up in Tree's shade that day, as I have so many times in my life, and as I was dropping off to sleep I remember saying to him, 'How lucky I am to have you.'"

And then in a voice so quiet I almost missed it, I heard her say, "I suppose that will never change."

After the children left, she turned to me and told me what I'd already guessed. "I've come to a decision," she said, and vanished from the clearing, leaving me alone with Tree, feeling stunned and useless.

Chapter Seven
SAYING GOOD-BYE

Since that day I'd been dreading her call. So when it came I was surprised at how bright she sounded. Still, after I hung up the phone I felt dull inside, the way you feel when you first realize your parents can't make your wishes come true, or keep the bad dreams at bay. Here it was, not even spring, and I had this year's tree lined up, but somehow I didn't feel like celebrating as I drove out to the convent.

It was one of those in-between days, not quite spring but no longer winter. The sun shone through the cold air, putting a much-needed sparkle on the brown and gray countryside, and flocks of birds flew overhead, their calls sounding like an announcement of the warm weather ahead. I like that time of year, when the earth's in a tug-of-war between old and new.

Sister Anthony met me at the convent and suggested we take a walk. I began to head toward the clearing, but she pointed me in another direction.

"I've already been to see Tree today," she said simply. I had the feeling she didn't want to see me around Tree. It was as if I was the messenger of doom.

Sister Anthony must have guessed how I was feeling, because she took special pains to be lively. We chatted about the spring Flower Show that was coming up, and she told me about a new rose hybrid she was experimenting with in her little greenhouse behind the convent.

We had walked quite a distance when she stopped by the edge of a little creek surrounded on all sides by trees and small hills. I had never been to this part of the property before.

"Lovely, isn't it?" said Sister Anthony. "This is the heart of Brush Creek."

We sat down together on a couple of large rocks whose flat surfaces had been nicely warmed by the sun.

"Tell me all about it," she said.

I looked at her blankly.

"Tree's journey," she said. "I want to know exactly what lies in store for him. And no cutting corners. I want to know everything, good and bad."

"Where do you want me to start?" I asked.

She thought for a minute.

"How will you get him there, to New York City?" she asked. "He's very tall."

I began to explain. I told her how the tree travels in a special trailer that's like an accordion. It can stretch out up to 100 feet. They say it can hold a tree 125 feet tall, though I've never seen it. The tallest tree that ever stood at Rockefeller Center was ninety feet, and that was back in 1948.

"What kind of a tree was that?" Sister Anthony asked.

"I believe it was a Norway spruce," I said.

"Hmmm," she said, then added. "How tall do you think Tree is?"

"Why, Sister Anthony," I said, laughing, "I think you're being a little competitive!"

She looked sheepish and smiled. My heart lightened, even though I knew this must be hard for her.

She wanted to know more. I think she wanted to make sure we knew what we were doing. Tree was her main concern and she needed to feel she was putting him in good hands.

But there was more to it than that. She had a natural curiosity about how things worked. She was interested in the mechanics of it, just exactly *how* you move a giant tree from here to there and keep it in one piece.

Once again, I found Sister Anthony shedding new light on something that had become old hat to me long ago. As I told her about the process, it struck me how amazing it really was.

"It takes weeks to get the tree ready," I said. "Then we get about twenty people and a giant hydraulic crane to help move the tree onto the trailer and then to put it up again at Rockefeller Center."

I was gathering momentum. "It gets really exciting on the trip into the city," I said. "The tree travels with a police escort at night, when traffic is light, like a president or a movie star, being whisked along in the biggest limousine in the world."

Sister Anthony was laughing out loud. "My goodness," she said. "You certainly make it sound thrilling."

She tweaked me. "All this from the man who hates Christmas!"

I was starting to feel relieved. This hadn't been painful at all.

Then she asked the one question I didn't want to answer.

It was innocent enough.

"How will you keep the branches from breaking?" she asked. "It's such a long way."

My relief evaporated. This wasn't going to be so easy after all.

"We, uh, truss the branches," I said casually.

Her eyebrows went up.

"Truss?" she asked.

I took a breath. "We position the crane alongside the tree and someone climbs up and ties each branch, one by one."

"One by one," she repeated. "That must take a long time."

I nodded. "It takes weeks."

"How tight do you tie the branches?" she asked.

I paused. "Pretty tight," I said.

She nodded.

I dreaded what was coming next.

"Do the branches ever break?" she asked.

Bingo! There was no avoiding it.

"Sometimes" I said. "Then we fix them."

"You *fix* them?" she said.

"We 'enhance' them," I said, and then immediately felt like kicking myself. "I mean, we add branches to replace the ones that get broken."

I expected her to get upset, maybe decide to leave Tree where he was.

But I should have known better.

"I can see why you would do that," she said slowly. "Something like fixing a broken arm."

She paused for a long while, then said, "Tell me again what the tree looks like when it's finished—all decorated and ready for show? I know I've heard you tell the children many times, but I want to hear it again."

I tried to drum up every fact I'd ever heard about the Rockefeller Christmas tree. I told her about how more than 25,000 bulbs of different colors were strung around the tree on five miles of electrical wire, and about the care the electricians took to wrap each branch separately.

Then I stopped. "I forgot," I said. "You've never seen the tree. This must not mean anything to you."

She shook her head. "No, go on. I can imagine it very well."

So I told her about the twelve angels, that Valerie Clarebout had sculpted for the Center's Channel Gardens years before, and how when you look down the middle of them you see the Christmas tree in the distance, like a cheerful apparition.

And I told her about the star. It was made in 1949 out of a material called Bakelite, and gives off a soft white glow. "It looks like a miracle," I said softly.

She took all of this in with a thoughtful look on her face, as if she were trying to conjure up the scene in her head. I offered to send her some photographs of Christmas trees from the past, but she didn't want them. "I think I understand now," was all she had to say about it.

We listened to the creek bubble along; suddenly it seemed very loud.

"Melting snow," said Sister Anthony absently.

"You know," she said, "I've always turned to Tree when something important was on my mind. Funny, I can't go to him now."

She stood up abruptly and waited for me to do the same. On the way back to the convent, she made it seem as if the only care she had in the world was whether her new roses were going to bloom.

❄ ❄ ❄

It snowed early that year. The fields were white the day my men and I went to get the tree. I hadn't seen Sister Anthony since spring, but my guys told me she was out there every day, watching them truss Tree's branches.

And now the time had come.

I knocked on the door of the convent. One of the younger nuns answered the door, and invited me inside to wait for Sister Frances.

I was shocked when I saw her. It had been quite a few years, now that I thought of it, since I had first met her and asked her about the tree. On my later visits, I'd generally made my way right out to the clearing.

The fullness had fallen from her frame. Her habit seemed to swallow her up. She moved very slowly, as if each step cost her something dear. I realized she must be close to ninety by now.

When she shook my hand, though, her grip was still strong.

"Good to see you," she said heartily, though her voice was thinner than I remembered.

"Sister Anthony's told me you two have had some nice talks over the years," she said. "I'm glad of that."

I didn't know what to say.

"Can you wait just a few minutes?" she asked. "All the nuns want to come out to give the tree a final blessing, if that won't hold you up too much?"

"Of course," I mumbled, holding onto my cap for dear life.

I saw the young nun who had answered the door go outside and disappear into a little stone building I hadn't noticed before. And suddenly the sound of bells ringing filled the air.

They all came.

Within minutes the yard was full of black habits. I hadn't realized so many nuns were staying at Brush Creek, though Sister Anthony told me there were always more than it seemed. In the middle was Sister Anthony, arm in arm with Sister Frances. They nodded at me and began to walk toward the clearing.

I went out front and told my men I'd meet them by the tree, then followed the nuns, staying just a little behind them. I felt like an intruder, but I couldn't help myself. I was drawn to their procession like a bird to a flock.

It was something I'll never forget, watching them walk through the fields, the hems of their habits turning white from the light dusting of snow on the ground.

The men had driven the trailer around and were waiting for us when we arrived. They were being a little rowdy, but when they saw the nuns approaching they quieted down real fast. You could see on their faces that they were moved by these nuns walking out there in the snow to say good-bye to their tree—especially since a lot of them were pretty old.

The drivers stood aside respectfully while the nuns said a prayer and sprinkled the tree with water. There were no speeches or anything like that. They just stood still for a few minutes and then gently began to sing with voices as clear and sweet as cold spring water.

As the last note died away, Sister Frances looked over at me and nodded.

"We're going to leave now," she said.

I saw her put her arm around Sister Anthony and heard her say, "Let's go inside."

Sister Anthony shook her head. "You go. I have to stay."

The other nuns had already started to walk back to the convent. I could see that Sister Frances really didn't want to leave Sister Anthony behind. She glanced over at me, but I just shrugged. Like I said, I'm better with trees than with people.

Sister Frances stood there, looking worried and suddenly very frail. She had quite a few years on Sister Anthony. In fact, they could have been mother and daughter, the current between them was so strong.

"It's cold," said Sister Anthony, smiling. "I'll stay by myself. I'll be all right."

Sister Frances looked at her closely and must have seen she was telling the truth. She gave her hand a little squeeze and left.

For someone who's never seen it, the way we cut down the trees is both amazing and awful at the same time. After all the weeks of preparation, the actual sawing only takes about two minutes, but, as I realized that day, that's a terribly long time to hear something you love getting cut open. The weird thing is that you can't really tell right away that anything has happened. The tree is suspended from a tall crane beforehand, so even after it's been cut it looks as if it's still standing.

I should have warned Sister Anthony. I saw the flash of hope on her face after the saw stopped and Tree didn't fall and I saw that hope disappear when we moved the tree from its stump and lowered it onto the trailer.

It was the moment when I traditionally count the rings on the stump to get an accurate idea of the tree's age.

I told Sister Anthony what I was about to do.

"Would you like to help me count?" I asked her.

Together we counted the rings. There were sixty-two.

"Just as I thought," said Sister Anthony. "Tree was just a little bit younger than me."

"You've both worn well," I said, not knowing what else to say.

Meanwhile, the men were measuring Tree's length.

"Eighty-two feet!" one of them called out.

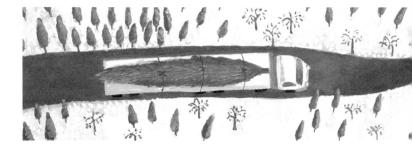

Sister Anthony was starting to look weary, but she was still game. "Only eighty-two feet!" she said. "And I was sure he'd be the tallest tree there ever was."

She took a deep breath. "Well," she said, "He'll be the most beautiful, of that I'm sure."

"No question about it," I said. There was so much I wanted to say to her, to thank her, to tell her we would take care of Tree. I just didn't know how. So I simply shook her hand and climbed into one of the trucks. As we drove away I could see her in the rearview mirror, a small lone figure waving good-bye.

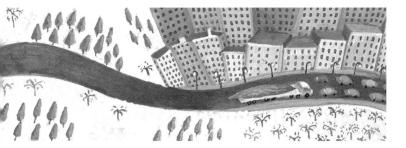

Chapter Eight

THE JOURNEY

 *I* made sure the powers that be at Rockefeller Center sent a special invitation to the Sisters of Brush Creek. It began, *We would be honored to have you present at the annual Christmas Tree Lighting Ceremony,* and was printed on a thick, cream-colored card, lettered in red and green type. Pretty classy.

Sister Frances called me a few days after she received it, full of excitement and thanks. She told me she'd set the card on a table in the vestibule and put out a sign-up sheet, to find out how many of the nuns wanted to go, and that it filled up with names in a day. Not only that, word had spread about the tree and the trip to the city—and many people wanted to come along, people who remembered the happy times they had spent under Sister Anthony's tree when they were young.

When Sister Frances added up the names of everyone who wanted to go, she realized there were far too many people for the convent van to carry. That didn't stop her, though. The convent had funds for special occasions, and she thought this was as good an occasion as she could imagine to spend some of that money. So she chartered a caravan of buses. She wanted to find out if I could arrange parking for them. No problem, I told her.

Then, two weeks later, she called again.

"I'm sorry to bother you," she said, "but I have a problem. I've been so busy running around preparing for the trip I didn't really notice how quiet Sister Anthony has been lately. Then, yesterday, I was looking over the list to see who had signed up and I realized someone was missing."

I interrupted. "She isn't coming?"

"Don't rush me, young man," said Sister Frances.

Obviously she was going to tell the story her way.

"The minute I realized she hadn't signed up I found her in the library and, I'm ashamed to say, spoke rather sharply to her."

I couldn't help smiling, imagining the showdown between these two.

"She asked me if something was wrong and I said, 'Yes, indeed there is. Why aren't you coming to Rockefeller Center with us?'

"I already knew the answer, of course. I must say, my heart went out to her, but I told her, 'There's a time to say good-bye.'

"You know what she said to me? 'I've already said good-bye.'

"At that moment she seemed like that sad little girl I'd seen almost sixty years ago, looking so lost and alone.

"'Are you sure?' I asked her. Well, I could just see from the look on her face that I wasn't going to change her mind."

There was silence.

"Sister Frances?" I said.

"Yes," she said, sounding somewhat startled. "Oh, yes. That's why I'm calling. I need you to come out to

Brush Creek the day of the tree lighting and bring Sister Anthony to Rockefeller Center yourself. You're the only one who can do it. I'm counting on you."

And then she hung up.

At first I wanted to call her back and tell her it was impossible. How could I spend the biggest day of my year driving all the way out to the middle of New Jersey and back? But my next thought was, how could I not?

When I arrived at Brush Creek the buses were already there. It was a long way into the city and the weather was poor for traveling. The temperature hovered around freezing, and the light snow that had begun to fall was wet and sloppy.

Despite the gloom outside, inside the convent felt festive. The main room was full of nuns, the townspeople who were going along and a huge number of children, some of whom I recognized as Sister Anthony's students.

Sister Frances was in her element, lining people up and telling them which bus to get on. You could see she was happiest when she held a clipboard in her hand.

When she saw me she didn't even say hello. She just nodded toward the back. "She's out in the greenhouse," she said. "She doesn't know you're coming."

"That's just great," I said to myself, kicking myself for coming on this fool's errand. What made me—or Sister Frances, for that matter—think I could change Sister Anthony's mind? And why should we try? Was it our place to decide how Sister Anthony should deal with the end of the most meaningful friendship she'd ever had? We couldn't even begin to understand the connection between her and Tree, and what it meant to have it broken.

I wanted to turn around and drive right back to New York, where I belonged. I didn't have it in me to be anyone's spiritual advisor—least of all a nun's.

While all of this was going through my mind Sister Frances was still tending to her list. When she saw I hadn't budged, she waved me away. "Go on," she said impatiently. "There isn't much time."

There was no answer when I knocked on the door of the greenhouse so I just went right on in. I could hear

Sister Anthony in the back, bustling about, humming to herself. As I started in her direction I knocked over a watering can.

Sister Anthony looked up with a start.

"What are you doing here?" she greeted me. "Isn't this your big day?"

"Nah," I said. "I'm already onto the next thing. I'm in the middle of planning the Spring Flower Show. As far as the tree goes, I'm more or less finished. There are a lot of other people who take over now."

I wasn't exactly lying, then again I wasn't exactly telling the truth either. It was true that the tree was in the hands of the electricians and the public relations people by now. But this was the first time I had ever been somewhere else on the big day: I was usually there prowling around, making sure everything was running smoothly.

She just looked at me, waiting.

"So, I heard you weren't coming," I said.

"That's right."

That was it. She wasn't going to make this easy. I took a deep breath.

"Look," I said, "I know it may be none of my business but I really think you should go see Tree."

She looked surprised. "I don't think I've ever heard you call him Tree before," she said.

I knew I had to keep going before I lost my nerve. Then it just all came out. "Sister Anthony, I don't know how to say this, exactly. I've spent most of my adult life trying to create beauty. I mean, that's my job—to create an impression, to wow people. Plants and trees are my tools, I use them like my computer and my Rolodex. At least that's what I've always told myself."

I couldn't think of what to say next. I felt like such a jerk. What was I doing?

Sister Anthony's eyes were sympathetic. And as she waited patiently for me to get my thoughts together, it occurred to me that she was helping me out once again, though I was the one who was supposed to be helping her.

"I guess what I'm trying to say is, well, that it's all a lie."
She looked puzzled. "What do you mean?"

"I mean it's not just a job, they're not just tools and I really do love what I do—and you've helped me see that. You and Tree. So please come with me. I'd like you to see where Tree has gone. It's important."

I stopped. I didn't know what else I could say.

Sister Anthony was silent.

"Please," I said.

❄ ❄ ❄

We didn't talk much on the drive into the city. I could see Sister Anthony taking in all of the ugliness as the beautiful countryside of rural New Jersey gave way to shopping malls and giant oil tanks and chimneys billowing smoke. It was all new since she had made her trip to Brush Creek so many years before.

Finally, we could see the city in the distance, but just barely. The air was thick with a frozen haze.

"On clear days the skyline just seems to sparkle," I said trying my best to sound cheerful.

Sister Anthony nodded politely.

"Is it familiar at all?" I asked her.

She shook her head. "Not at all."

I was thinking we should just turn around and go back. This was a terrible mistake. What would she make of all the hoopla which was part of the tree-lighting ceremony, with its big-name performers and politicians and TV cameras? I was afraid that if the crowds didn't overwhelm her, the entertainment would.

The traffic was murderous. We crawled across town. She kept shaking her head. "I don't remember anything," she said. "Nothing."

Then in a sad voice, she said, "This is what I feared most of all, you know."

"What's that?" I asked.

"I've always had a good feeling about New York, something I've never been able to put my finger on. Just a general kind of warmth," she said. "But this—this isn't it!"

I looked out of the window and tried to imagine how it looked to her: It was all gray—gray people huddled over as they made their way across gray streets that were bordered by gray buildings. The only thing that wasn't gray was the noise—big red blasts of horns blowing and walkers and drivers cursing at one another and of course the ever-present sirens.

I wished that we could have driven down Fifth Avenue. At least then she'd have a chance to see the Christmas decorations and the angels lighting the path to the tree. But I knew the traffic would be a nightmare so we stopped near Sixth Avenue and made our way across Fiftieth Street, pushing through the mob that

surrounded the area that we'd roped off for the nuns. Sister Anthony didn't complain but she looked miserable—tiny and frail in the crush and the cold. For the first time since I'd met her, she seemed old.

"It'll be great when we get there, you'll see," I said, elbowing people aside to make a path for her.

We finally made it. I got a glimpse of Sister Frances and her group but before I had a chance to look up, to see if the tree was actually there, one of my guys grabbed me by the arm.

"We've been looking all over for you," he yelled and took me with him.

By the time I'd taken care of whatever it was, I couldn't make my way back to Sister Anthony. I caught her eye from a distance and waved at her helplessly as the ceremony began. She smiled and waved back, a bit too heartily to be convincing.

It all happened so quickly. There were the speeches and the singing and the tree was lit.

I didn't pay attention to any of it. I kept my eyes on Sister Anthony, trying to make out what she was thinking. At first she looked troubled.

"She shouldn't have come," I muttered to myself.

Then something happened. Her face lit up and she looked years younger, almost like a child. She was smiling as she lifted her hand toward the tree and her lips moved. I'm pretty sure she said, "Good-bye, my friend."

When it was over I tried to reach her. But the crowd closed in on me and by the time I made my way over to where the nuns had stood they were gone.

Chapter Nine
THE CHRISTMAS TREE

Over the next few weeks I kept meaning to get out to Brush Creek for a visit. But things caught up with me, the way they always do. As usual I was busy growling about next year's Christmas tree and what a pain in the neck the whole thing was.

Then I got her letter. It arrived at the office one day when I was in a particularly bad mood. When my secretary buzzed me to let me know the helicopter pilot was waiting for me, I barked at her. "Let him wait!" I said.

I closed the door and began to read.

❆ ❆ ❆

I was right. The crowds and the entertainment had all seemed overwhelming. She was wishing she hadn't come. She was frightened. Worst of all, she didn't recognize her tree in that place, surrounded by huge buildings instead of the sky, its branches weighed down with a brightness that all seemed false.

Then the lights came on and way up at the top, the star.

Here. I'll let her tell you the rest.

I was overcome by the memory of a star from long ago. Suddenly I remembered that I had been there before, at that very place, with my father and that he had said the strangest thing. "The city is our jewel—beautiful yet hard."

I remember at the time I was a little frightened by his voice. There was a depth of sorrow there that I had never heard before. Later I realized he knew what I didn't, that he was dying.

He must have sensed that I was scared, because when he spoke again I heard the gentle tone I was used to.

"See that star, Anna, there at the very top?" he said. "It's there to remind us of the beauty, even when all we feel is the hardness."

Standing there with Sister Frances and the others, I finally understood what my father was trying to tell me, and how much it must have hurt him, knowing that he wouldn't be able to teach me all the things he wanted to. I felt so proud of him, remembering that moment, and so lucky to have it come back to me. My fears just disappeared.

I looked around and saw the happiness on the faces of the people who were dear to me, and the strangers, too. I looked for you, but couldn't find you in the crowd. But the crowd no longer scared me because I could see that the people in it were doing just what my father had said to do. They were looking for the beauty.

And they found it. My Tree gave it to them.

He was beautiful, wasn't he? And I was able to see him, underneath all his finery. It was my Tree after all.

Everyone here at Brush Creek is still talking about how exciting it all was. Otherwise, everything is pretty much back to normal. I've been reading about a new variety of tomato I want to try this summer, and puttering around the greenhouse. I'll be glad when it warms up and I can get out in the garden again.

You must come and visit us soon. I've told this year's group of children all about the Christmas tree and about the clever man who chooses it. They think that must be a wonderful job to have. Just come out to the clearing any day in the early afternoon. You'll find me there, next to the little Norway spruce the children and I planted this week.

You were right to make me go. You're a good friend, and for that I thank you.

I had to sit there for quite some time before I could move. My head and my heart were full. Finally, I put the letter in my desk and walked out of my office, feeling strangely light.

I saw my secretary staring at me.

"Well, you look a little happier," she said. "What did you do? Take a nap?"

"Why shouldn't I look happy," I said. "I'm going out to find a Christmas tree."

About the Author

JULIE SALAMON is the author of *Facing the Wind*, *The Devil's Candy*, *The Net of Dreams*, and *White Lies*. Formerly a reporter and film critic for *The Wall Street Journal*, she is now a critic for *The New York Times*. She lives in New York City.

About the Illustrator

JILL WEBER is a freelance illustrator and book designer. Her illustrations have appeared in more than a dozen books for children and adults. Her most recent works include *Expectations: Best-Kept Secrets Every New Mother Should Know*, *Harpo's Gold*, and the soon-to-be-released *Hear the Angels Sing*. She lives on Frajil Farms, in New Hampshire.